MY FAKE BIRTHDAY

MY FAKE BIRTHDAY

Alok Singh

GenNext Publication

ISBN : 978-93-8022-299-8

Price : ₹ 150

First Published, 2016

Published by

GenNext Publications
5, Ansari Road
Daryaganj, New Delhi-110002
Phones: 9811692060
E-mail: gennext@hotmail.com

Printed at: G. Print Process, Delhi.

Cataloging in Publication Data—DK
Courtesy: D.K. Agencies (P) Ltd. <docinfo@dkagencies.com>

Singh, Alok, author.
My fake birthday / Alok Singh.
pages cm
ISBN 9789380222998

1. Singh, Alok. 2. College students—India—Lucknow—Biography. 3. Love. I. Title.

LA1153.7.S56 2016 DDC 378.19809542 23

Acknowledgement and True Words from Author

Dear Readers,

Your Author belongs to a medium class family of District Azamgarh in Uttar Pradesh. I don't want to show my qualification here because I firmly believe that sometimes your life teaches you in a better way than your degree and job. I have been writing my diary from my childhood to express my thoughts and emotions. I have gone through the various phases of my life which inspired me to write my emotions to express it to you people.

I believe that there is always a ray of hope to live in your bad times. No one knows about tomorrow. So have faith in God and start living. Everybody is effected by the different flavors of love at different ages. Some express and some enjoy hiding their own while listening and enjoying other's. Though it is a passing phase of every young mind but sometime it makes such a deep impact on our mind that it's not possible to erase from our heart and mind. This book is inspired by true happenings and I am sure that it will win core of your heart.

I thought of many times to publish my writings but felt scared of writing industry just like a man who enjoy acting but forgets thinking of huge bollywood industry. I believe in originality and I am sure that my book is not away from it. I don't want to write lenthy so read the book and enjoy. Your reward to me would be your feedback on my mail id:

alok0airforce@gmail.com.

Dedicated to

My Parents and siblings

All my readers who believe in love in true sense

My beloved wife

My little sweet baby (Shaurya Pratap Singh)

My friends who motivated me to write this book

My Sincere Thanks To:

My beloved wife Priya Raj Singh who kept on asking about the book and listened my writings on day to day basis on phone.

My Siblings, Ashutosh, Ankita and Akash who expressed there excitement to read it in turn motivating me to expedite.

My Editors Saurabh and Shreya (Director, Ministry of MSME) who read the first complete soft copy of this book.

My friends who helped me at different stages Mr and Mrs Munesh Nehra, Mr and Mrs Bhoop Singh, Mr and Mrs Satish Sharma, Shyam Sundar Yadav, Sudheer Kumar, Sanjeev Kumar, Dharmendra Singh, Anand Singh, Abhishek Singh, Yashpal Singh, Rahul Singh & Saurabh.

10:15 a.m., 14th October, last year (2014), University of Lucknow, Department of Statistics.

It was my first day in college. A class of 34 students was all set to attend the lecture by Professor Sheetal Dixit, a lady with a great personality having height of 5′9′′. She was very stylish and used to wear gown, adding more gravity to her personality. She used to keep 3 to 4 perfumes inside her Honda city car. A great benefit what I got that I came to know the brand of perfumes by regularly noticing insider her car during break hours.

She entered in the class. We all stood up to our respective seats. She asked the class to sit but I was only glaring at her. My wild imagination reached to the thought that she could perfectly play the role of the professor in any student-professor love story.

She started with the chapter of probability. At 11:05 a.m. by my watch, another grey color Hyundai Accent car arrived in the parking as it was visible from lecture room. A girl of about 5′8′′ height, wearing suit and light blue color jeans and medium height skin color sandals came out and approached to our lecture room. She was having diary with brown cover, written "MY LIFE MY CHOICES" over it with fluorescent color and pink color stationary purse.

She asked ma'am to enter in the class.

"Yes come in. What is your name?" Mam asked.

"Ritika"

"Why are you late?"

"Mam, my car suddenly stopped on the way due to some technical glitches. I called the mechanic and got it rectified. That's why I got late" She replied.

"Ok, take your seat" Mam said. She thanked mam and entered in the class with a very beautiful smile on her more beautiful face.

Alongwith the class, I came to know her name. My attention had diverted to her from Sheetal Dixit. I wanted her to come and sit alongwith me but there were no vacant seat on any side of me. I cursed my fate and gave a strinking look to Chintamani who was sitting adjacent to me. He strangely looked at me and asked me what happened. I avoided him and started looking at her.

In our class, boys were sitting from the third row keeping blank the first two rows for girls. I had got seat in third row. She took seat in second row just in front of me. The flight of my eyes changed its destination from Sheetal Mam to Ritika and landed on her neck. It was long and one of the most beautiful neck I had seen in my life.

The fragrance of Sheetal Mam's perfume had lost and her's spread through every nerves of my body. It worked as a virus which made my brain and heart to hang on her. It became difficult to concentrate on Mam's lecture. I started noticing her writing, her sitting posture and most of the time her neck.

She had worn a black thread in her neck. I was sure that some culprit would have seen her beautiful neck with evil eye. She would have pain in it and then her old grandmother would have advised her to wear this. I felt envious about the culprit.

I don't know which brand of shampoo provides such type of facility that her hairs were looking too much smooth and separated with each other. I started imaging in my mind about a romantic story in which actor first smells the fragrance of actress's hairs then keeps it aside and finally kisses all over it after which actress closes her eyes.

Sheetal mam continued her lecture on probability but I could hardly understand anything except probability of my relationship with her. Mam finished her lecture by 11:30 am.

On my bench we were three boys. The right most commented "Very nice perfume Ritika." I felt awkward. She pretended not to listen and left the class.

"Excuse me, what's your name?" I asked.

"Hello! I am Chintamani from Varanasi. You are new to this class, I think?" He said.

"Yes, It is my first day in class. You should not comment on a girl like this, she is from our class man" I said.

"Great friend, sympathy and safety for girls from the very first day…! control yourself buddy and grow up. You are in L.U. campus, not in your school. Girls want compliments. If not tell me why she had spread such a nice perfume?"

"Yes. Girls are fashion pro and want compliments but she is not an usual one. She is my girl and only I have all the authority in this world to like her and compliment her..." I answered him in my mind but I kept silent and left the class.

Then, I went to faculty of maths. I attended the lecture and returned to my room at new Hyderabad colony, in front of university. Shyam Sundar from Sahjhanpur and Saurabh from Barabanki were staying on rent in the same building where I. Shyam was preparing for banking and Saurabh for SSC. We all were sharing a common kitchen. They had taken admission in coaching institutes and were pursuing their graduation from KTM College.

I forgot to introduce myself to you. I belonged to a medium class family of Azamgarh district in U.P. which is about 300 Km. away from Lucknow. I had two younger brothers and a sister and I was the eldest. When I was about to leave my home to board the bus to Lucknow, my father told me;

"You are going to live alone. You will have to take every decision of your life on your own. We are from middle class family. You know better than me how does our home run in my little salary. The only thing which I have got is respect in our society. Never do anything which hurts me and your mom."

I remembered every sentences of my father. I had decided to work hard and never let my parents feel bad because of me. I had also decided not to be in love till I am not successful. But that unique and unrestrained attraction toward Ritika was unparalled. I was losing control on myself and getting more and more attracted towards her. At the same time, I started worrying because I was crossing limits set by myself. My mind was full of thoughts and every good thought related to her was countered by the bad one generated by me itself.

Shyam, Saurabh and I were used to had dinner together. We had our dinner by 10:15 pm. and went for walk having normal gossips.

"Hey Dear ..you looking little bit worried?" asked Saurabh.

I instantly replied, "No". This was a sign that I was thinking something seriously and yes, I was.

"Hey man ...you got your girl on the very first day…must be thinking about her..yeaaa? Shyam chucked on me.

I denied him outwardly but could not deny the very true saying," "True love cannot be found where it does not exists..nor can it be hidden where it does".

I went on my bed to sleep but could not. "I should focus on my career and do not go ahead with her.. But She is so sweet that I can not afford to loose her..." I was discussing it again and again in my mind. After one hour of insight discussion, the feeling of love prevailed conditionally. The condition being not to disturb my studies. I started thinking how to move further to get her close. I landed up in on a plan to ask her for notes of stats of previous classes. I managed to sleep by 12:30 pm.

The Day Next

I was used to start my day with previous day's happenings. So automatically my mood was showing sign of happiness or sadness dependent on the day past.

I was very excited as well as terrified for that day plan. "Where should be the starting point? What should I say and how to say?" My thought process started giving negative signals on these lines. I was scared of her refusal to give her notes. As it was my first action plan I wanted to be very much cautious. I left my bed and stood in front of mirror and said:

"Hello Ritika, It's me Raghav. It is my second day in the class. I don't have notes of previous class. You must have prepared those notes. Can you please give me yours so that, I may copy?"

My mind started repeating these four sentences. It was repeated for at least 50 times in next one hour. My curiosity and fear were increasing with the time.

I could not remember when I got refreshed, took bath and had tea. These four sentences were hammering my mind. I took out new clothes and dressed up myself in best possible manner. I walked fast to university to catch the seat just behind the girl's row.

I met there Chintamani outside the lecture room and told;

"Where r u from and where do you live?" I asked.

"I live in Krishna Nagar. One more thing, your pretty girl also lives in my colony. She has a very beautiful home. Her father is an IRS officer."

Chinta gave me little bit comfort by saying "Your pretty girl". I thought that he will not try her at least. But being a daughter of hi profile father scared me.

We both sat on the same seats as yesterday. My eyes were waiting for Ritika to come. Her car reached in the parking. She had worn a grey color top and black color jeans. A new thing was a goggle with large glasses reflecting seven colors. She was looking more beautiful than yesterday. She entered the room and searched for a vacant seat. I was praying to God to see her sitting on the vacant seat in front of me but she took seat in left row second bench.

I got tensed. My mind stopped working for some moments and heartbeat increased. I doubted of her smelling my intentions. My mind, heart and my eyes were at her only.

Sheetal mam came inside and the whole class was filled with the fragrance of mam's perfume. She started the lecture on Correlation. But I was thinking about the action plan only. Suddenly, Mam made an eye contact with me and asked;

"Are you new to my class?"

"Yes mam, Myself Raghav from Azamgarh. Due to some family issues, I could not come early. But now I will attend the class regularly."

The whole class moved their heads towards me. I made an eye contact to Mam and then Ritika. Mam said;

"No issue but take notes from someone and copy it. If you got stuck anywhere, approach me and I will help you. But do not miss class today onwards."

I nodded in acceptance.

I thought as God was favoring me. It was the first time when my eyes met with her. She made an eye contact with me for fraction of second then diverted towards Mam.

Every nerve of my mind and body relaxed. I took a deep breath. This introduction made me to cut the three sentences as introduction part was over. I missed fragrance of Ritika's perfume. I missed watching her beautiful neck closely. Mam completed her lecture and left the class.

Ritika stood up and asked a boy standing in the row just behind him;

"Manav, you did not come yesterday. Was there any problem?"

"Yes, I went to airport to receive my sister coming from Bengaluru." He said.

My insight burnt. I felt envious of him. They both left the class together having conversation. I approached Ritika, but I could not make courage to ask her for note due to Manav being with her. I saw Chinta approaching me.

"You walked so fast and approached them?" Chinta asked.

"Yes, actually I wanted to ask her for previous class notes."

"Why are you asking for her. Take mine." He said.

'No thanks, I want her notes only.' I said.

'That's what I wanted to listen from you. I smelled your intentions from the very first day.' He said.

'Oh! Am I so easy to understand? Do you know the guy with whom she was?' I said.

'Yes, he is son of our Science faculty dean, Mr Shashank Sen Gupta. Their parents know each other'

My tension increased with my blood pressure. I felt more and more envious of Manav. Chinta said;

'Don't worry. Manav is not interest in her.'

'But what about Ritika?' I asked.

'I am not sure of her but I don't feel so'

Chinta made me comfortable. He did the job just apposite to his name Chinta (Worry). But I felt as a villain making entry in my love story from beginning. I walked towards canteen with Chinta and had tea. I felt upset of my today's plan being unsuccessful. But I felt different when I remembered the moment when my eyes met with her. I walked to my room with low mood.

Saurabh was good in cooking. He had prepared a fried rice and dal. I remembered my mother's advice;

'Take sufficient and healthy food. Never be lazy in preparing it. Avoid the food from outside as it is not hygienic.'

I had sufficient food and normal gossips with Shyam and Saurabh.

The day three (16th October);

I woke up by 07:15 am. The first thought came in my mind was about the villain of my love story. I was so envious of him that he was coming into my thoughts in equal frequencies as Ritika's. Though he was not interested in her but Ritika's simple conversation with him made villain for me. I left the bed fast before a bulk of thought could strike in my mind.

I prepared tea for all of us. I always loved making and having tea with others. I tapped on the head of Shyam and told;

'Woke up man, Come out of dream. Its 07:45 am.'

He opened his eyes and said;

'Hey buddy, I love you more than my sister. At my home, She prepares tea for me and here you. The only difference is that my sister brings tea after I woke up as she knows that I love sleeping. You should adjust your time.'

'See his attitude, I am telling you that if you will not start waking up early, we will pour water on your bed.' Saurabh said.

'You continue man. I am sure you will get the award of punctuality one day. I don't need that.' Shyam reacted.

I smiled and a bulk of happiness ran throughout my mind and body. I thought that if my friends love me, a day will come when she (Ritika) will also love me. Saurabh always used to leave his bed by 05:30 am. Needless to say, Saurabh was disciplined, sensitive and serious while Shyam was bit of casual nature.

I dressed up myself and left the room. Today we and Chinta sat on the seat just behind where she sat yesterday. I was eagerly waiting for her to come. Sheetal mam entered the class and started her lecture. She and Manav, both were absent from the class. My suspicious mind started thinking that surely they will be together today and will be roaming somewhere or planning to watch movie together. I asked to Chinta;

'Do you have any idea that why she did not come today?'

'Not exactly but I saw her going somewhere by her car at around 10:00 pm' He said.

I doubted of some miss happening with her. I imagined myself of being with her in misfortunes. My mind was not stable. I thought that my plan is going to fail today also. I could hardly concentrate on mam's lecture. She finished the lecture and left. I walked out of room with Chinta with tensed mind.

As soon we reached outside of faculty, I saw Manav and Ritika standing below Peepal tree with her car parked near by them. I felt upset watching Manav with Ritika. They were asking everyone to stop and gather. It is said that people use their mind more often where it needs not to be used at all. I am also a human being. How can I keep myself aside? My doubt had taken shape in real terms. I felt like my heart is broken. My love story, moreover my life story, had finished even before start. Chinta realised my tension and told;

'Something is burning, I can smell'

I made a fake smile and moved ahead. I pretended of not to notice them and moved ahead. Then, she raised her voice and said;

'Raghav, please come here, here is something for all of us.'

My whole body felt of being in chilled water after facing the hottest sun. I took a deep breath. My heart started pumping at normal rate.

'Hi! And sorry, I couldn't notice you.'

Life gives you sometimes such situation in which u tell just opposite of your inside. Everyone gathered below the Peepal tree and paid attention of her. I was the most excited and thrilled person in that gathering.

'Hello everybody! Please don't think me as a leader of student union. Today is my birthday. I want to share this special day of my life with all of you. I have cake inside my car. I ordered it at late night and shop opened late in the morning so I missed the class and made the Manav too. I wanted him to accompany me to make some arrangements.'

Everyone had smile on their faces. I was also happy except accepting of Manav to accompany her. Ritika took out the cake from car and kept it on the roundel made on the root of the Peepal tree. We all made the circle. She kept the 18th year's candle over it. Manav lit it up.

Ritika extinguished the candles and everybody started singing the happy birthday song. I also sung it with replacing Ritika to 'My Ritika' in my mind. She again seek attention of everyone and told;

'Thank you everybody. Thank you so much. Please do not go anywhere after eating the cake. We all will go the canteen; there is arrangement of samosa and tea for all of us.'

Ritika distributed the cake to girls and Manav to boys. It was chocolate flavored cake and too much tasty. After that everybody started moving toward canteen. Manav was engaged in conversation with Desh Deepak (A student from our class) and Ritika was moving with Jyoti (A girl from our class). I don't know that there was nicotine in cake or not but my mind worked at faster rate. I thought that she will not refuse me to give her notes today. I approached her and said;

'Hello Ritika'

'Yes Raghav'

'The cake was too tasty.

'Thank you'

'Actually, I don't have the previous notes of Mam's classes. Can you give me yours?'

'Oh! I am really sorry; I was in haste today to reach the shop yearly, so I forgot my diary at home. I can give it to you tomorrow.'

'No issue, I will take it tomorrow from you. Thanks.'

" No issue my dream. Whole time of this world is yours only. I can wait for your notes but I will take them from you only. Not tomorrow then day after tomorrow....". I said to Ritika in my thoughts.

Then I took a deep breath and started walking slowly. Every nerve of my body was smiling. I wanted time to stop for sometime and let me live the moment again and again.

I felt myself in comfort zone. I did it as per my plan. I thanked God for all favors. My job was over. It was now her turn to remember and give it to me. We all reached to the canteen and managed to accommodate in less space inside it. Canteen boys served the stuffs to everybody. Manav and Ritika took at the last. Everybody was engaged in conversation with each other.

My sensitive mind, you can say more sensitive went back and remembered my name coming out of her throat to her tongue and finally on her lips. I loved her way of calling my name. I introduced myself only once to the class and she remembered my name. I was in dilemma that whether her memory was too sharp or she was interested. As I was in love, I accepted the second one.

I felt something different after remembering her calling me in her raised voice 'Raghav please come here.' I felt like she knows me from long times and she has right to call me in any way. These four words started coming in my mind repeatedly. I felt her of being very close to me.

Everybody finished tea and samosa. Ritika seek the attention of everybody again and said;

'I want to thank everyone from core of my heart to join me today. We will have more fun in my next birthday. I want to make memories from my collage life. Thank you so much.'

I remembered those four words at least for 100 times till evening. I felt excitement after thinking of giving me her diary tomorrow.

Saurabh cooked 'mutter paneer' and myself chapati's for dinner. We had our dinner discussing about our families. Shyam's job was to wash the pots. I managed to sleep by 11:30 pm.

17th October,

I woke up by 07:15 am and left the room by 09:30 in excitement for faculty. Ritika entered in the class. He noticed me. She sat on the middle row, second bench. I had taken seat just behind her. Sheetal mam started her lecture. I could not escape myself from watching her silky hairs and beautiful neck. I smelled her fragrance. I imagined my lips being on her neck.

Today, Manav was not present in the class. I kept my eyes shifting from mam to her and vice versa. I was eagerly waiting Sheetal mam to finish her lecture. She finished the lecture and left the class by saying;

'Some veterans will arrive in our university on 20th. So I will not be available for class. If u people want, u can come and study here. Lecture room will be opened.'

As soon mam left the class, Ritika stood up, turned towards me and said;

'Hi Raghav, It's my diary. You can keep it with you. My writing is not so good. You would need to concentrate more to understand.'

I smiled and opened her diary.

'It's not so poor to understand. I can manage.' I said.

'Means it is poor?'

I laughed and she followed me.

'It's great that you at least know your negative.' I said.

'Can you give me a favor?' She asked.

'Of course, Say'

'I and Manav missed the class on my birthday. So can you write it in my diary?'

"Definitely, I will write it. I had attended the class that day"

'Thanks and Bye.'

'Bye'

I can't explain the quantum of happiness, I got. This short conversation made me comfortable with her. I wanted her to tell that I can write all the three year's note on her diary if she allows me. I loved her funny way of talking with me.

Two words which were pinching me were 'I and Manav.' I wanted earthquake to come, drowning everything except me and her then she will not have option other than living with me. She will have to utter my name only.

How this love makes a man so selfish, I came to know. I forgot the condition of my family in earthquake. I forgot my close friends and wanted them to die. Moreover, I forgot my survival with her in earthquake. This is the ultimate truth of love that you want to get your love at any cost. That's why it is so beautiful and called blind.

I walked fast and went straight to my room with all happiness jumping inside my heart. I imagined myself being a captain of a team, winning a crucial match of tournament. I locked the door from inside. I picked the diary with both hands. I touched her name written over it by my eyelids, by my nose and finally kissed it many times. I thanked God for favoring me to reach my love. I kept it on my heart and pressed it to be closer. But suddenly my wraith asked me in my dreams, " Raghav, what are you doing? You are not here to do these stupid things. You are here to fulfill dreams of your parents. You are loosing control of your mind."

Somebody knocked the door and I woke up strangely and opened the door. Saurabh was there. Shyam had gone to his relative home residing in lucknow and returning in the evening so we two had lunch. Everything let it be water gave me a delicious taste.

Saurabh's eyes went on the diary. He exclaimed with surprise;

'Hey Raghav! It's very pretty diary. Ritika? Who is she? '

I smiled and said 'My classmate man.'

" Oho classmate's diary on your bed. And your smile is adding something more to it"

'Oh,You can say her my friend, but I am not sure what does she thing for me.'

'But, My sixth sense, which is always right, is saying that my dear friend Mr Raghav is in love. Hip hip hurrreyyy. But dear, You must make her realise your feelings."

'I don't know dear what actually love is; but I am going through some different phase of my life now a days. I became lost somewhere, whenever I think of her.' I narrated him my four days story and my conversation with my wraith in my wild dreams.

'It's normal dear. But I think it is the most beautiful phase of your life. You are in love and only thing you have to do is to make proper balance of things so that your studies do not get disturbed. Do not loose control of your mind. But dear make sure that she also has feelings for you, otherwise it is very dangerous. I have experiences from my life to guide you a little bit on this stage. It's a type of ghost. Be cautious.' I nodded my head and went for sleep with a heavy heart.

In the evening, Saurabh prepared tea and asked Shyam to join to us. Saurabh told the hole story to Shyam and again cautioned me to follow my mind not my heart.

'But she is not a type of girl you are thinking, I said.

'Every girls looks initially like this only. The reality comes out when you try to get close to her' Saurabh told.

'Dude, You should follow your heart and let it go on and on.' Shyam said.

'Don't listen to this lazy man. You should go and take bath first' Saurabh reacted.

'C'mon man, when my body will realise, I will definitely go. Then only I can enjoy it. Why should I force myself and take stress for it.' Shyam said.

'But we are not a son of section engineer in railway like you .We need to take stress for our future' Saurabh said.

I tried to settle their arguments. Then I went to a photocopy shop to make a copy of her notes including cover page and bought a gel pen. I wanted her to impress her by my writing. I forgot to tell you that I had taken part in district level writing competition, during my schooling and I was good in playing cricket. I wrote her diary in my best possible manner.

We all had tea together in the evening. Nicotine of the tea did its job and an exciting idea stroked in my mind. I thought of celebrating my birthday. I had never done this before. Even I did not remember the exact date. It was not in my family's culture. I wanted to be in level of her standards. If you are in love with a hi profile girl, it happens most of the time. I wanted to give a party to my whole class.

Though it was not for whole class. I wanted to show her my levels and to show her that I also want to make memories from my collage life. I remembered that Sheetal mam will not be available on 20th. So I can make arrangements in lecture room.

I was nervous and confused how would I organise the things for the event. To make myself confident, I thought of celebrating it on night of 19th with Shyam and Saurabh at our room to make practice of cutting the cake and extinguishing the candles.

I was so excited that I could not control myself.

'On 20th, I will be having my birthday. We will enjoy the cake on 19th night only. I have to take two cakes, one for us and one for my class' I said.

Shyam smelled my intentions.

'Wow that's great. So you want your beautiful girl to taste your birthday cake?'

I smiled and said 'I will be very happy to be with her on my birthday (Actually fake birthday).'

We discussed for ordering cake from a bakery shop in JK Bakers at IT Crossing. Generally your friends manage the cake for your birthday and you manage the party but I became so responsible in love. That I thought if they will forget to bring the cake, I will not be able to do my practice in turn I will not be confident in front of her. So I went to shop and ordered two chocolate flavored cakes, one for rehearsal and another for the special day.

18th October

I took her diary and kissed again. I went to the faculty and stood outside the faculty near peepal tree. I was waiting for her. One more idea clicked in my mind. I thought of taking her help to bring the cake tomorrow from bakery shop (03 Km away from campus Approx.). Bringing the cake was secondary issue but I wanted to be with her on my birthday.

It was 10:30 am by my watch but her car did not arrive. I was in much tension because if she will not come today then tomorrow too as Sheetal mam would not come for class. My plan would be failed. I was getting more and more embarrassed with time approaching for class.

Meanwhile, Sheetal mam's car arrived in the parking. I walked fast to enter inside the class before she enters. I was not feeling well. I was just looking towards mam but my mind was somewhere else. It had become usual practice for me that whenever I used to be more excited for something, exactly opposite happened and reverse current of depression flew at the same voltage of excitement stopping my motor of the brain.

I closed my eyes, remembered God and said;

'Please favor me once more'

Mam finished her lecture with reminding us that she will not come on 20th (Monday) for class. I had decided to inform everybody for tomorrow's event and thought of catching Chintamani to inform her.

'Hello, everybody on 20th I will be having my birthday. As there will not be lecture, we will make arrangements inside the room only. Please do come. I will be very happy in making memories with you all' I said.

I left the class with very low heart and tensed mind. My eyes suddenly diverted towards a Hyundai Aceent car parked little away from our faculty. I observed Ritika sitting on the driving seat. I approached. She stepped out.

'Hi' she said.

'Hello! Is everything alright?' I said

'Almost, my mom was not feeling well actually. I took him to the doctor'

'Okay, how she is now?'

'Better'

'Okay. It's your diary. I have completed it. Let it be with me.'

She gone through the pages and said;

'OMG! It's beautiful writing. Is it yours?'

'No, there is a puppy in my colony, who loves to write on girl's diary. So I went to him and told to write it down.'

'Okay thank him from my side when you meet and tell that I will give him more to write' she said with smiling face.

'Leave your diary with me only. I will write down today's lecture also.' I said.

'No…Thanks. I will write it on my own but I want your note book.'

I gave her my notebook.

'I want to say something but I am in hesitation.' I said.

Her face expression changed. She looked embarrassed and tensed as if I had said to her 'I love you Ritika' tough I desperately wanted to say that only.

'Tell.' She said.

'Actually, I am having my birthday on Monday. I want to give a little party to our class. I have ordered cake and petties to a bakery shop at IT Crossing. So I want you to meet me there in the morning. I want you to help me in bringing stuffs to the class.'

Her face and mood came to normal position. She smiled.

'Raghav, It's your birthday. I will be happy in helping you and making you happy. When you will reach to shop?'

'About 10:00 am, because it's opening time'

'Okay, then I will catch you there, after that we will come to faculty'

'Okay'

'I have to leave now.' she said.

'See u then. Bye'

'Bye'

'I love u Ritika. You are so sweet.' My mind, heart and my body coordinated each other to repeat these four words inside my soul. My love for her increased 10 times more. I loved her of being so helpful and soft hearted. I loved her of being so simple in spite of her hi profile family. Love is beautiful. All problems of this world can be solved with help of love only. People come and go but love remains forever. I went to the canteen and ordered samosa and tea for 35 peoples.

I came to my room. I remembered her stepping out of car, her entire conversation with me and her smile.

I and Saurabh went to the bakery shop in the evening. I ordered the 3 KG chocolate flavored cake for tomorrow and bought half kg for tomorrow's tonight.

Shopkeeper asked me for birthday candle. My mind went in dilemma. Ritika had celebrated her 18th birthday. As per my actual birth year my 18th year was also running but I remembered the husband-wife age culture followed in our society in which husband should be one or two year elder of wife. One more thought came in my mind that it was my fake birthday. Coming in same month and placing same year candle may place one's mind in doubt. If you are copying someone you must have some deviations otherwise you will be caught.

Shopkeeper observed my dilemma and said;

'Sir it's not your birthday?'

'No someone else' I said.

I asked him to give the 19th year's candle.

'Raghav, you don't remember your birth year?' Saurabh smiled and asked.

'Actually, I was counting the total years.' I pretended.

'Your math is very poor.'

I felt under confident. We returned to our room with cake, mutter and paneer for dinner. Saurabh cooked the paneer and myself chapati's. I was good in making the round chapati's but if I failed to make first then you can see the different maps of world in each chapatis.

We had our dinner by 10:30 pm. We went to our rooms to relax.

On 19th night, Though it was the responsibility of Saurabh and Shyam to wake up me for cutting the cake but I could not sleep thinking that they may forget.

They did their job and took me inside the Shyam's room.

I cut the cake after lightening the candle. They hugged me and sung the song. Shyam placed the cake on my whole face and after that I did the same on their faces.

I finished my practice and washed the face. I did not want to be late tomorrow. I tried to sleep but hardly, I could.

20th October 15

I woke up by 06:45 am. They both wished me again. I told them that we would have dinner outside.

'First go and let your pretty girl to eat your birthday cake. I have special perfume for you to impress your pretty girl.' Shyam said.

'That's great; I want to dress up myself in my best way.' I said.

Shyam gave me the perfume. I used it on my shirt. I borrowed a fast track watch from him which gave me an executive look. I took auto and reached the bakery shop by 09:30 am.

Boys from the shop were cleaning it. Man on the counter ensured me of delivery by 10:10 am. I walked on the road with excitement to meet her.

I paid the money. Ritika arrived by 10:20 am. She was looking awesome. Today, she had worn a yellowish suit and blue jeans.

'Many Many happy returns of the day Raghav ' She wished.

'Thanks' I said.

'I am sorry; I got little bit late due to my some personal needs.' She said.

'No need of sorry, I just paid the money.' I said.

'So let's take and move.' She said.

I placed the cake on the rear seats and sat on front. I felt like being in the best place of the world. I wanted the world to notice that I am with my love. I felt so romantic.

'So where are you from?' I asked.

'Basically from Sultanpur, my father is an IRS officer. He works here so we live in our home at Krishnangar.'

'Okay.' I said.

'What about you?' she asked.

'I am from Azamgarh' I said.

'Oh, you are from very dangerous place. Some terrorists were caught from your district. You might be knowing.'

'Yes, but it does not meant that everyone in my city is like them only.'

'Don't take it on your heart.'

'Do I look like?'

'No you are so innocent, that's why I am with you.'

I relaxed thinking her perception for me.

'You are from a rich family, so why did you choose to go for B. Sc.?' I asked.

'Actually, my mother is a psychiatric patient. She needs more care. My father is too much busy in his job. So, I don't want to leave her.'

'It's very heartening. You are really a great daughter. Now a days, nobody wants to spoil their career in taking care of parents.'

(That's why I love you, I thought)

'I don't think for my future. I am just trying to do my best in present scenario.'

'That's great'

'Where do you live here?'

'Just 02 km away from our campus, opposite to our university, there is a new Hyderabad colony.'

'Okay'

'When did your mother become sick?' I asked.

'From last three years. She thinks too much and not able to concentrate on her routine.'

'I should not ask but may I know the reasons of being her like this?'

'It's a long story. I will tell you letter on. I don't want you to feel sad today. You should be happy.'

'It's fine'

We kept silent for some time. By the time we reached to the faculty. I took out the cake. Ritika helped me with taking the candles and match box. People wished me. I saw Manav inside the class. Ritika approached him and started talking with him. My insight burnt again. Though she gave me so much favor but I did not her to talk with others. I needed her attentions. I wanted her to be mine only.

Chintamani arranged the table and cake in front of lecture room. Everyone gave attentions. Ritika lightened the candle of 19th year and asked me to start. I extinguished the candles. Everybody clapped and sung the song. Ritika helped me in cutting the cake in pieces and distributing it to everyone.

That picture perfect I imagined in my dreams. I with Ritika only were present in the room and she was wishing and asking me to cut the cake on that very special occasion. After cutting the cake I grabbed her in my arms and put my lips on her.

I and Chintamani went to the canteen and brought samosa and tea. We served it to everyone. People made theirselves busy in conversation. There were many gifts also. Ritika went to her car and took out her gift. I seek attention of everybody and said;

'I am very much thankful to everyone. Though it was not lecture today but you all attended it. I felt very happy and it will be stored in my memory for throughout my life. Thanks a lot.'

Everybody dispersed after that I went to her and said;

'Thank you very much; I liked your company today.'

'Not required, I feel happy in making others happy. So I do it for my own.'

'That's great'

'I have to leave now.'

'Ok; you should. Bye.'

'Bye'

I walked to my room with jumping feet. Today I imagined myself, being a captain of team qualified for semifinals. I was much excited to open the gift by Ritika. Shyam entered inside my room, hugged me and said;

'How was your day buddy?'

'The best one of my life bro'

'Your queen tasted your cake?'

'Yes, here is a gift from her. You can open it.'

It was a beautiful diary with two sticker of smiles and written 'SMILE PLEASE'.

'OMG!!! It's so beautiful. You are so lucky man.'

Meanwhile Saurabh also entered inside the room hearing our conversation. We all three opened the gift one by one. I thought of telling them the truth. Though, I felt embarrassment but I managed to say;

'I don't want to hide anything from you guys now. Actually It was not my actual birthday.'

Shyam and Saurabh wondered.

'Not your birthday? What do you mean?' Shyam asked.

'I have never celebrated birthday before. I did it to show her that I am in her level to get close to her' I said.

'Then what about yesterday night' Saurabh asked.

'I did it do rehearsal before my actual performance'

They both laughed and I followed.

'You are unique piece in this world Raghav. People should take ideas from you to reach their fiancés.' Saurabh said.

'But I am very much happy today. It's more than actual birthday for me.' I said.

'Wow. So tell us the story what happened today? '

I narrated them the whole event.

'You have literally lost your senses in love. Control yourself. Speedy vehicles are vulnerable to accident.' Saurabh said.

'Don't listen to him man. Just follow your heart and move on. Life is too short. You must keep yourself doing crazy things.' Shyam objected.

They ate chocolates from one of my birthday present and left the room. I took the diary presented by Ritika and touched it to my heart and kissed the smiles over it. I remembered the every moment of today. I lost myself thinking of her.

'We are going for dinner outside today, Was this also fake?' Saurabh asked with smiling face.

'C'mon, it's more than my birthday. We are definitely going. I want you both to be in my every emotion.' I said.

'Oh that's great. I know a restaurant in Aliganj who provides very hygienic and tasty food.' Saurabh said.

'So let's go' I said.

We had dinner outside but my mind was with her only.

07 DAYS LATER

I continued attending lectures and conversation with Ritika. But my desires were increasing day by day. I wanted my relation to expedite. I wanted to be more close to her. Almighty favored me and I got one more chance.

Our seniors approached us to celebrate and give us fresher's party. They asked us to take part in singing, dancing, skits etc. We discussed to celebrate in a memorable way. Jyoti, a girl from Nalanda Bihar, living in Lucknow, having attractive eyes was in awesome in singing. She told that she will sing a song. Three boys (Ravi, Vikrant & Akash) from same school during their schooling decided for a group song. Sahaj, a boy from Sitapur agreed for solo dance.

Ritika informed us that she will do the anchoring. She asked that if anybody can accompany her in Hindi then it will be more attractive.

Though, I had never performed any act on the stage but I did not want to leave this golden opportunity. I thought it as a super natural power favoring me to reach my love.

I had done schooling from Hindi medium so speaking Hindi was not an issue but facing the stage worried me. Before anybody snatches my golden opportunity, I said;

'I can do it in Hindi.'

'Very nice, we will write our dialogues as per the programme and then practice it', She said.

'Rite'

Though, I was nervous of facing the stage but more excited of sitting with her and doing practices. If someone else would do anchoring with her, It would be hell for me to be there watching her with someone else on the stage.

The date was finalised as 30th Oct. We had one week for practice. We and Ritika made the list of all programme discussing with seniors and sequences of it. Ritika asked me to sit with her to prepare the speech and list. She had worn sleeveless black color suit with designs over it and white salvar.

She took out her sandals and sat on the floor near podium and asked me to sit. I sat with her leaving 10 to 15 Cms gap between us. She took out the A4 size papers from her diary and started writing.

(1) Saraswati vandana by Seema, Shruti and Vidushi.

(2) Solo song by Jyoti Srivastava.

(3) Solo song by Sahaj.

I interrupted and placed my right index finger on the second programme over the paper. My shoulder touched her shoulder's. My wrist met with her. My mind and my heart lost somewhere. It was a different feeling which intoxicated my whole body. I felt like drunken. My mind was not on the paper but I managed to say;

'Don't you think that dance should be first and after that song. It will vibrate the whole hall filling it with lots of energy. The stage should rock first. Then song by Jyoti will be more enjoyable.'

I saw her face to make an eye contact but she did not. She diverted her eyes from paper and watched in front. I had not seen her face like this.

'I think so but let me complete it roughly then we can change it later on.' She said in low vice.

I kept my shoulder aside but the virus which hanged my system was doing its job. She again started writing at slower speed.

(4) Skit by Shakti, Amit and Abhishek.

(5) Solo dance by Somi Rai.

This time, I knowingly made my shoulders to touch her's. Her pen stopped for some movement. I kept watching on her paper pretending to feeling normal.

'Tell me the next' She asked.

My mind was somewhere else. I thought of her being in same mood.

'(5) Group dance by Sheetal, Saumya and Ragini'

She wrote it down and then I stood and said;

'Let's go to the coffee shop. I am feeling exhausted.'

'No be here only, until we complete the whole list atleast.'

I don't know what was the reason, either she was concentrated on her work or she was also intoxicated, I loved her stopping me like she has right on mc.

I tried to keep my shoulder's aside. I felt her feeling the gap between it. I was just feeling the ultimate intoxication of love. I wanted to tell her that she was the most beautiful girl of the world. I wanted to tell her that I can't imagine my life without her.

Our heart talked to each other silently. She managed to complete the list and said;

'Let's go and have coffee. Then rest we will do tomorrow'

'Oh thanks, let's go' I said in tired mood.

We ordered two coffees, sitting facing each other. My eyes met with her and hanged on her. She diverted her eyes towards the waiter. We had it discussing about the party.

Next day, we attended the class and after that we all discussed about the arrangements. Then Ritika asked;

'Mr. Raghav, are u ready to accompany me in writing our speech'

'Of course, but there is class here' I said.

'So let's search for a vacant place' she said.

We walked towards the department of philosophy and sat beside each other on cemented chairs below the banyan tree.

She had worn a kurti and black jeans. We folded our one leg and sat facing each other keeping the diary between us. She started writing.

Our foreheads were very close to each other. I was able to smell the fragrance of her hair shampoo. I leaned little more towards her and our forehead touched each other's. A liquid of romance flown throughout my body. I lost my mind somewhere else. I could not hear the sounds of birds over tree. Her pen stopped and face expression changed. I thought it as a best position of Yoga where my mind was fully concentrated at her only.

After some time, She unfolded her leg and sat straight. I copied her. She again started writing.

'Our Respected Dean Mr Shashank Sen Gupta, our HOD Mr Yashwant Singh, Distingushed Guest, My seniors and My colleagues, A very good morning and I welcome you all on this special function. I want to start this function with a motivational story.......

There was a shopkeeper who used to make samosa and tea at his little wood made shop. But he used to open his shop from 4 pm to 6 pm only. People rush to his shop between these two hours due to its delicious taste. Rest of the time he used to roam here and there in his village.

One day he was sitting under the mango tree with his wife and drinking sugarcane juice. A young boy working in a multinational company from his village came and asked…

"Baba why do you open your shop only for two hours."

'What If I open it for whole day?' Old man said.

'You can earn more money' Boy said.

'What would happen then' Old Man said.

'You can have better shop and earn more money' Boy replied.

'What would happen then' Old Man said.

'You can have boys to work at your shop' Boy said.

'What would I do then' Old Man said.

'You can have peaceful life and enjoy' Boy said.

'Is not that I am doing now.' Old man said.

Morale of the story was that to enjoy our lives we don't need too much money and power.

So make this occasion enjoyable I and Raghav will call our participants one by one.They have great caliber and unique talents. They will rock the floor by their performances. But without worship nothing should be started. So let's start with Saraswati vandana by Akansha, Arpita and Ruchi.'

Then, I helped her in writing my Hindi speech between the programmes. One programme was to be announced in English by her and next in Hindi by me. Following these sequence, we managed to complete it.

We kept silent for some movement after this. I placed my right hand over her left and kept aside. She was not reacted. Then I again placed my hands and made a loose grip.

I imagined it as a best movement of life when I held the hands of my love. My eyes wanted to be closed and be with this movement only. I wanted time to stop here forever. Though we did not talk but our souls were talking each other. I tried to make eye contact but she did not. She continued to look in front.

A group of students approached us. She removed her hands. When they went inside the faculty, I asked;

'What do you want from your life?'

'I always concentrate on my deeds. I try to do best in my present. I never thought to achieve or get from my life' she said.

'That's great. Are you inspired by holy book 'Geeta'?'

'Yes but not only because of its being holy but I find it logical also.'

'Okay. You seemed to be mature enough.' I said

She smiled and said 'Hey! But don't' treat me as an old lady having lot of experiences from her life. I am young and having enthusiasm to do anything.'

I smiled and she again asked;

'What about you?'

'I just want to be with you holding your hands forever' (I wanted to tell her).

'I want to be a hero in everyone's eyes. I want to do something different by which people remember me' I could say.

'Oh! You want that people should hang your long photos in their homes and offices.' She said.

'Not at all, I just want to be in people's heart (in your heart first, I thought).'

'That's nice. If you have an option of selecting a friend in which one follow his heart and another mind, which one will you select?'

'I will decline both and search for third one who knows to keep balance between two. I believe in keeping balance in life.'

'Very clever. You look so innocent but your mind is not so. But I will go with mind follower because I believe in logics'.

'Means, you don't have heart inside.'

'Of course I have. That's why I am alive. But I just want it to continue its job of pumping my bloods.'

'If you will not follow it, why it will follow you? She will do its job in its own way. Sometimes it will increase your B.P. and sometimes lover it.'

She smiled and I followed her. I found it difficult to understand her. She was following her heart by not resisting me when I hold her hands and saying just contrary to it. I felt scared of her following logics in future with me which might destroy our present relationship.

'Let's go and have a cup of tea.' I said.

'If you insist, I have to'

We went to the canteen and ordered tea with samosa.

'You told me that you will tell your long story about your mom. What is it?' I asked.

'C'mon concentrate on the coming event. I will tell you later, I promise.' She said.

'Okay, Its fine.'

We left the campus after making the two copies of speech. She told me to practice at room. I felt very comfortable with her today.

We met next day. We found a vacant class in arts faculty. First, Ritika stood on the Dias and started the speech. I sat in front of her to judge her. She had worn a grey top and black trouser. A fast track watch was giving her very friendly look.

She continued her speech and I continued watching her beautiful eyes. I could hardly concentrate on texts of speech. She was rotating her eyes to every corner of the room to make eye contact with audience but my eyes had hanged on her. I felt intoxication again.

She finished her speech then I clapped and said;

'Well done, Miss Ritika.'

'Thank you Mr, It's your turn now. Go and let me sit now.'

I went to the Dias and started. I was nervous. I continued the speech watching her. She interrupted.

'Hey! You have to face everybody. Don't look to me only. Rotate your head.'

'On the final day, you will not be with me. Then I will rotate it. Today, I will see you only.'

She laughed and told me to continue.

I finished the speech and we sat together after that. Our shoulder touched each other's in very short span of time.

'Nice, but you need to be more energetic while calling the participants on the stage.' She advised.

'Okay, I got it.' I said.

'Relax for some time and after that we will have one more practice.'

'I will practice again only if you will promise me to tell your story after it.'

'No, concentrate on your anchoring first.'

I made a serious look and kept silent.

'What happened?' She asked.

I did not react.

'Okay, I promise, I will tell you.' She said.

After that we did one more practice and sat moving our heads slightly to face each other. She started,

'Actually Raghav, my father is very careless about us. He just keep busy himself with his job and in earning money.

My parent's marriage was an arranged marriage but my father had an affair with a girl named 'Shruti Yadav' from varanasi since his collage. Due to different communities, family of girl was not agreed for marriage and she was married to another boy.

After two years of her marriage my father got selected for IRS. Due to pressure from my grandfather and relatives, my father got married to mom after two years of selection. My father and Shruti continued meeting each other.

My father had physical relationship with my mom in early stage of marriage. But my mom received a call of her on our basic phone. She told that she is talking from papa's office. But mom doubted. She asked my maternal uncle who was working in Kanpur at BSNL office to take out the monthly call details of papa's cell.

Then after lot of enquiries mom came to know about her. Mom started quarrelling with my father almost every day. My father told my mom that if she wanted to take divorce she could.

My mom got hearted from inside. She was carrying me inside so she tried to keep normal. After my birth, mom kept her busy with me. My father continued meeting her. My mom saw her messages on papa's cell many times.

She became habitual of facing the daily drama. Mom tried to adjust but continued going in depression. She fell sick and case of 'Major depressive disorder with anxiety.' My father did not care for my mother. My maternal uncle took care of my mother. Due to continued stress, she was not recovered and started forgetting small thing initially. When I was of 05 years she went in coma.

My father was took care of me initially. He used to bring toys for me. When I grew up then I took the fever of my mom seeing her condition. I talked hardly to my father one day. He did not reply but stopped talking with me.

'I had seen Shruti. She is very beautiful. Once my mom was admitted she came to our home. But I never told my mom.'

Tears started coming out from her eyes.

'Hey common stop it. I was not knowing that you story is so tragic otherwise I would not have asked you to tell.' I said.

I wanted to wipe her tears but I could not make courage. I just placed my hands over her. More drops started coming out of her eyes when I asked her to stop.

It happens when you have a heavy heart and someone ask you to stop your tears, your emotion jumps to its maximum level and pain releases in the form of water at faster rate. I thought saying "Stop" at this movement as 'Start'.

I wanted to hug her tightly to make her comfortable. I wanted to take all her pains inside my heart. I wanted to tell her that need not to worry as I was with her.

'C'mon 'Ritika let's go and have tea.' I said.

We went to the canteen and sat facing each other.

'My mother has faced much in her life.' She said.

'Yes, it's very heartening.' I said.

'I wanted to cure my mother. I wanted to see her normal but the doctor told me that it may take long time. The doctor advised me to keep her away of stress.

'Okay untill your father will not start behaving properly, it will be very difficult.'

'I know but don't want to quarrel with him. It will make our family environment more stressful. I am moving with a ray of hope when he will himself feel to take care of my mom.'

'Okay'

'Raghav, I learned driving at my 12th standard so that I can take my mother regularly to doctor.'

'That's great. You are too responsible.'

'But Remember, I am not an old lady. I am of your age only.' she smiled and told.

Meanwhile canteen boy brought the tea and we had it. I felt sad of her tragic story but happy as well thinking that she had started sharing her emotions with me.

'Can, I have your cell number?' I asked.

'You ask so innocently that It is more difficult for me to refuse you. But if you promise not to miss use it.'

'I promise.'

'One more thing, never give it to anyone in any condition. I have faced lot of problems and it's my third contact number.'

'I can understand. Keep faith on me. I will not miss use it.'

We exchanged our numbers and left the campus.

We continued our practices for rest of the day. I purchased khaki color trouser and red black combination shirt for anchoring. A day before the party we had rehearsal.

Party timing was 10:00 am. Everybody reached including Sheetal mam. Everybody was waiting for our dean Mr Shashank Sen Gupta. His car arrived by 10:15. Ritika came on the stage and asked our dean to lit the Diya.

Ritika had worn a green color sari in modern style. She was looking so beautiful that some people started taking pictures on the stage. I felt uncomfortable. I did not want my love's photograph in other's camera and phone. I kept watching her on the stage. When first programme started, she came and sat near me in the dressing room.

'You are looking so beautiful today.' I said.

'Thanks Mr.'

After that I went on the stage. My legs were trembling but I managed to control. We kept on going as per plan. Programmes were finished by 12:30. Now there was arrangement of petties, pastries, other snacks, tea and coffee. Our seniors asked our dean to start. I and Ritika were together having plates of stuffs. People came and congratulated both of us saying 'Energetic Anchoring'. A research scholar approached us and said;

'Well anchoring Ritika and very nice costumes. You are looking awesome.'

'Thank you sir' she said.

'Where are you from by the way?' He asked.

'From Sultanpur district but my family lives here only.' she said.

'I am also from Sultanpur. Where is your home in Sultanpur?' he asked.

'02 Km away from bus station.' she said.

'Okay, I live near chowk.'

'Okay sir'

'Can I have your contact number?' he asked.

I lost my patience and raised my voice;

'Why do you want her contact number?'

'Who are you by the way?' he asked.

'What do you want me to be?' I replied.

People near us started starring at us.

'Raghav please be cool.' She interrupted.

'She is from my city. I am just asking her number. What do you have a problem?' he asked.

'I know well about people of your type.' I said.

'Raghav, please stop.' She raised her voice and told.

'I will see you later on' he said.

'Sir please go' she said.

After that Ritika dumped her plate, and stood near the girls from my class. Award for Mr Fresher and Mrs Fresher was announced by Sheetal mam. Jyoti and Sahaj from our class collected the trophy from our dean.

I wanted to interact with her but she started her car and left the place. I was not feeling comfortable and not able to understand what to do. I took auto and went to my room with lots of thought coming in my mind. After lot of internal discussion, I thought of saying her sorry by sending her message.

I typed 'Hi Ritika! It's me Raghav. I am sorry for whatever happened today.'

My heart started pumping at faster rate but I could manage to click send button. I got a delivery report. I was very excited and tensed as well. I waited for half an hour but did not receive any message. I doubted for delivery. I kept on watching my mobile. Though it is displayed on front screen when you receive message but every time I opened the inbox and checked for unread messages. It happens, when you are nervous, you lose your faith on everything.

I send the message again and got delivery. Pressure on my head started increasing with time. I thought of losing Ritika by my silly mistake. I thought her of ignoring me even after opening my message. After one hour my screen flashed with '1 message received.' I opened it in excitement but it was service message from BSNL.

'Mai akeli hun, Karen chatpati masaledar batein. Call 50007055. Rs 3/minute) (I am lonely. Do stuffed talk.)'

Just after 10 minute I received one more message.

'Hi, I was busy so I could not reply you. Its ok but your aggressive behavior scared me.'

'You are not aware of intentions of such boys.' I said.

'I was not going to give her my number. You should not behave instantly like this.'

'Okay but I felt uncomfortable at that movement and lost my patience.'

'You should have control. I know to deal with such boys. You know people will have wrong ideas about you and me.'

'I will not show you such type of behavior in future.'

'It's ok. See you Bye.'

'Bye.'

I felt much comfortable after this. I felt throwing 100 kg of load after carrying it for long time. I thought of God pressing 'Undo' button in my life. I brought cold drink and snacks and served it to Shyam and Saurabh with cheers.

I started sending her one forward message daily. I continued interaction with her in the class. I wanted to raise my standards. I wanted to learn four wheeler driving and wear branded clothes to impress her by all means. But money provided by my home was not sufficient for this.

I joined a coaching institute to take class of 10th standard students to teach them math's. Coaching head offered me Rs 2500 for two hrs. of class daily. I felt God favoring me. I wanted to work hard to get His more favors. I took class for 15 days and asked the coaching head Mr Sahni to give me advance of Rs 1000 I joined a driving school.

I tried to concentrate on my studies too. I kept myself busy throughout the day. Winter vacation started in December last. I went to my home and relaxed there.

My mind diverted from Ritika. I felt happy at home. My grandmother asked me each and everything about my life in Lucknow. She asked me that which time I go to university for classes, which time I cook food and about my roommates.

My mom advised me to take fruits and healthy diet. First time in my life, I felt like guest in my own home. She prepared good dishes for me daily which she used to prepare when some guest arrive at our home. She wanted me to eat more and more.

I slept 3 to 4 hrs. during day. I was not able to sleep at night. 'A jobless mind is devil's one'. I thought of sending her message.

'Hey, I am at my home. How's your life there.' I typed and sent.

'That's great. How are uncle and aunty?'

'All are happy having me. They talk to me more and more.'

'Wow. You are adorable son. When will you come back?'

'On 10th Jan'

'Ok, so enjoy with your family and take care of them.'

'Okay, you take care of your mom.'

'Yes, Bye good night'

'Bye'

When only one day was left for leaving my home, I felt homesick. I did not want to leave my sweet mom and grandmother. I touched my mother's feet to leave. Drops of water started coming out of her eyes. I could hardly control myself but managed to leave. I reached Lucknow and met to Shyam and Saurabh. I shared my mother's handmade sweets and snacks with them.

I met with Ritika after the class.

'After long time, it's good to see you' I said.

'Okay, How was your vacation.'

'Very crazy, I was a guest in my own home.'

She smiled,

'It happens. You studied?'

'Not at all, I could not open my book even.'

'Same here. You are looking healthy.'

'It's a magic of my mom's food'

'That's great. You should take care of your health here also.'

'It's very difficult.'

'C'mon Even this life is difficult but still we survive.'

'Okay'

I loved her noticing my health and advise to take care of it.

ONE MONTH LATER

We were having gossips at my room.

'How is your beautiful girl' Shyam asked.

'Concentrated on her studies now days.' I said.

'Your relationship with her is in progress?'

'No dear, It's Constant.'

'Why don't you propose her?'

'I am scared of her rejection. I will lose everything then.'

'Means, You are happy to continue as her friend. C'mon she may be having more friends like you.'

'May be but she never told me about even single one.'

'Girls never tell. They get the world's best happiness observing more and more boys behind them.'

'But I don't want to take risk.'

'No risk, no gain man.'

Thoughts started striking in my mind. I was not able to make courage to propose her face to face. I thought of sending her message. Sometimes, I thought of taking risk but felt afraid of her rejection. I took my cell and typed a message. I wrote and deleted. I wrote something different and again deleted. I wrote for at least 10 times, then I could finalise.'

'Hi Ritika, I don't know whether you will like it or not. If you will accept it, I would feel to be in heaven otherwise my life would be hell. I like you more than my life. Do you?'

I closed my eyes and managed to press the send button. My heart beat increased at its max level. I got delivery report. I was watching the screen with attention. A gun of thought started killing my mind. I did not get any reply in next one hour. I opened the message and resent it. I again got a delivery report but she did not reply. Shyam observed my tension and asked.

'You seem to be restless. What happened?'

I showed him my cell. He wondered;

'You are so fast buddy.'

'But, she has not replied.' I said.

'Wait, it's not so easy for a girl to reply on these issues.'

'But what if she will not accept?'

'C'mon man, your life will not stop by leaving a girl. Another will make entry in your life.'

'It's so easy for you to say but I know I will lose everything. I love her only.'

'It's your first crush?'

'Yes, first and last. I can't imagine another girl taking her place.'

'Listen, it happens only once. Thereafter you will never take it seriously.'

'I can't live without her.'

'Don't be so negative. Hope for the best and be ready for the worst.'

I was not feeling appetite, though I did not had my breakfast and lunch. I felt my life to be on edge and about to ruin. I again typed a message by 10:30 pm,

'Please reply me. I am not feeling comfortable.'

About 20 minutes later, I received a message.

'I am feeling sleepy, I will see you tomorrow.'

I felt little bit comfortable but one thing worried me was her late reply. Different thoughts at different angles were fighting each other in my mind but negatives were more dominant. I thought if God would have provided shutdown button then I could have relaxed till morning. My system was started hanging due to less memory space available in my brain's ram.

I went in the balcony. I prayed God to favor me once more watching in the sky. I took water and poured on my head. I felt relaxed for some time. I went again to my bed. It was 1:30 am by my watch. I tried to sleep but could not. I again came to balcony and saw a star falling. I had heard from people that if you take a wish seeing a falling star, your wish gets fulfilled. I wished Ritika to be mine. It happens when you are in difficult situation, you start believing on super natural powers.

I thought about unfair thing in our normal life. A boy can't sleep after proposing a girl and thinks for whole night about her while a girl get very easy sleep. I could hardly sleep and left the bed by 0500 am. First I went to Hanuman Mandir and worshiped for favor. A controversial thought came in my mind that 'Hanuman Ji like celibacy. How does he will allow me to get a girl. But I worshiped with my true heart.' I came to room and distributed the Prasad to Shyam and Saurabh.

I went to the faculty and waited for her. She came and told me to meet after the class. It becomes very difficult to face a girl after proposing her. My heart beat continued to beat at faster rate throughout the class. My legs trembled as soon as class got over. I could manage to approach her. We went to a lonely place. I could not look at her eyes. She told;

'Listen, I am not here to be in love. I don't believe in it, so I don't want to waste my time in it. Don't talk to me here after. I can't even imagine of you having such a feelings for me.'

'Ritika, I can't live without you.' I said.

'Mr, it's not a movie going on here. Be in your own senses.'

'But what about things going between us for last three months.'

'What happened between us? Tell me. I am surprised.'

I could not tell anything except keeping patience. Until and unless you don't have anything in black and white, you can't claim.

'Ritika please, don't be so cruel to me' I begged.

'I didn't want to be but you made me so.'

'I can't even imagine my life without you.'

'C'mon try to understand, you are away from your home to study. I don't want my time to waste in it.'

'I will never make any hindrance in your studies. If you will not accept, my life will stop here only.'

'Don't be so sentimental. I don't have such feelings for you.'

'I don't want to be but I am not able to come out of it.'

'Actually, I am already in a relationship.'

'Please don't lie for God shake'

'It's true, I did not want to tell you but you made me so.'

'But why you did not told to me earlier.'

'Listen, we never discussed on these issues.'

'With Manav?'

'No, but now I don't want to tell you anymore.'

'You cheated me.'

'I could not smell your intentions otherwise, I would have told you earlier.'

'Being in love with someone is a wrong intention?'

'I don't want to discuss. I am getting late. I have to leave now.'

She left but I kept standing there only. I felt of being lonely in the world. My body, heart and my mind trembled. I wanted to scream loudly to release the pressure. Everything looked around me seemed to be of no worth. I lost faith on Hanuman Ji. I lost faith on falling star. I felt scared of facing her. I walked to my room. My face expressed everything to Shyam and Saurabh. I told them about happenings.

Shyam consoled,

'Don't take so much tension. God might have reserved more beautiful girl than her for you.'

'But I wanted her only, I din't want more beautiful.'

'See it's you first time, that's why you are so much tense. Now you will enjoy it.'

'I don't want to enjoy with any other girl. I love her only.'

'Okay but don't think of losing everything here only. Know body knows what is going to happen in future.'

He tried to console me but I couldn't understand even a single logic. Nobody was thereto understand pressure on my head. If somebody has even a little bit physical damage, people ask everything about it but nobody cares for internal damage because its quantity can't be measured, It can be felt only by the bearer.

I wanted the society to have specialist doctor for the losers in love. I found it as a one of the chronic diseases of the world. It was a most difficult time of my life. I felt scared after thinking my future career and life there. I wanted to leave that place to forget everything.

I did not want to think of her. But more I avoided more I landed up in remembering her. I felt helpless. I imagined if God would have provided format option for my mind's hard disc. I wanted to divert my mind from her but I find it as a most difficult task of my life and hardly I could.

Life had become challenge for me. My appetite lost. I forced the food to go inside to survive. I tried to sleep but I scared of thoughts coming in my mind. I came in the balcony and had water. Shyam advised me to smoke. I tried but I coughed. I again tried and again coughed. Nicotine worked for some movement.

Though, I hated the person of smoking and drinking habits, but now I had started my own. I felt sacred of new directions of my life but I needed it to keep myself stable. It was a tough task to face her but I decided to do it. I wanted to do everything what my mind was suggesting not the poor heart, by making it dominant. I decided to improve myself. Though it was difficult to do but I decided to do everything which was difficult for me. It was the only option I left with to survive.

I faced her in the class and canteen sometimes. Though it was difficult but, I had started taking challenge. I started studying my books. I learned driving. Though my mind was going towards her only but I kept trying. I never sat in the row, just behind the girls. I wanted to delete her contact from my cell but I could not because a ray of hope was still existing there in my heart and expecting some miracle to happen.

Our exams started. I attended with satisfactory level. Then I left Lucknow in the month of may for two months. My mind diverted from her. My life started coming to a normal routine. I kept myself busy at home in playing cricket., roaming here and there and meeting with friends.

There was 'Ritika beauty parlor' just in front of my colony. It reminded me always about her whenever I went out of colony. I wanted to crash the board badly and throw it in garbage. I did not want anything making me to remember her.

II YEAR

17th August This Year, (2015)

I managed to score 63 per cent in first year. I had diverted my mind from her keeping myself busy at home. I was scared of facing her again, so I did not want to come but I was not having choice other than coming back to Lucknow.

I met with Shyam and Saurabh and started going to faculty. She did not attend the class till 25th August. Though I wanted to ask Chintamani about her but I did not as I had started following my mind. She came on 28th August in the class. Our eyes met for fraction of second then I diverted. Sheetal mam asked us to solve a question written on board and show her tomorrow.

I solved the question with the help of a senior. The next day, I was sitting just behind her. Jyoti asked my notebook to see the solution. Ritika took my notebook and wrote it on her notebook. But she did not return me directly and asked Jyoti to return it.

I heard good news from our HOD.

'There is a inter department cricket tournament. There will be total 07 teams. It will start from 04 September. Two matches will be played daily. Your seniors have been informed. Sanchit, you may be knowing, a research scholar, will be the Captain. People interested may give their name to him.' He said.

'I want to participate sir' I said in haste.

'What's your name?'

'Sir, Raghav Singh'

'What do you do well?'

'Sir I can bat well and keep as well.'

'Okay meet to Sanchit after the class.'

Though, I would have given my name directly to Sanchit sir but I wanted to make her feel that I was doing well in my life without her. Muneesh and Anand also went with me and met to Sanchit sir. I wanted to continue with her by this attitude only. God favored me this time.

We had 03 hrs practice daily. Our HOD sometimes visited to make our morale high. A day before our first match he came to our class and said;

'Tomorrow we will play our first match against department of computer science. Everybody has to be there by 10:00 am for cheer up.'

I felt so happy thinking that Ritika will also witness the match now. It was best chance to show her my capabilities. I was too much excited to play well.

Next day, we had practice in the morning. Everybody gathered in the ground to cheer up including her. We lost the toss and apposite team decided to bat first. They scored 95 runs in 15 overs. I was doing keeping. Muneesh bowled well and took 04 wickets.

Now it was our turn to bat. Our openers could make the partnership of 19 runs in four overs. I went for the batting. I imagined myself being a star player to whom audience was excited to watch. I wanted to be a hero in her heart. I wanted to show her that she had refused to a guy who had caliber in many regions and she knew little about him.

In excitement , I played on long off in the air but It was my luck that player could not take it and went for four. Chintamani Screamed;

'C'mon Raghav, Carry on.'

I again played a boundary in same over on third man area. People cheered up and said;

'Great Shot. One more, One More.'

I saw her. She was also clapping and looking excited. My morale went in the seventh sky. I felt of winning the match at this movement only. I wanted to convert every ball into the boundary. But the captain asked me to play with patience. I and sanchit sir added 59 runs in next 9 overs then I caught behind. 17 runs were required in last two overs. In second last over, Anand scored 10 runs and then 07 runs in first three balls of last over. We won. Boys and girls from our class came and said;

'Well batting bro, you played very nicely, Wow Buddy u rocked. etc.'

Ritika came to me and said,

'You are hidden warrior Raghav, You play very nice.'

'Thanks' I said as I didn't care.

I avoided her and went towards our HOD. She smelled my intentions and went towards girls from our class with sad face. I felt of God favoring me in exploring my talent to show her.

'Keep on going with same Josh. Well done. There will be more hurdles in coming matches.' HOD said.

'I will try to do my best sir.'

Then I walked to my room with very happy mood today. I remembered her compliment 'hidden warrior'. I wanted to tell her that everything is hidden inside my heart. I wanted to tell that just accept me, I will show u my all hidden talents. I wanted to tell that I need you in my every highs and lows but could not because I was a hidden warrior.

We won 04 matches out of 06. I scored well in three. We qualified for semifinal with department of business administration. We won it by 05 wickets. Then reached to final which was scheduled on 16 Sep against faculty of arts. Everybody from my class was too excited to support to win. Ritika also came to cheer up. Our VC Mr Jagdeesh Singh also arrived to witness final match and to distribute the award there after with proctor.

We won the toss and decided to field first. Muneesh took his first wicket on first ball. Whole team managed to score 67 runs in 14.1 overs. Our inning started and we won the match in 10.4 overs. Captain Sanchit sir scored well and gave easy win. I could score only 08 runs this time. Our team collected the trophy from our V.C. along with our HOD. I also got a medal for best scorer of tournament. After that photography started.

I was standing beside her. I wanted my medals to give her and tell her that it's all because of her rejection; otherwise I would not have done well. After that I went to the room. I showed victory sign to Shyam and Saurabh. I was happier to win her heart rather than final match. I wanted to celebrate it.

At evening we and Shyam planned to booze. Shyam arranged the bear, we and Saurabh arranged the dinner and real juice for Saurabh. I had not drink beer before. I tried a sip and felt its bitterness from top to bottom.

'How people drink it so easily man. I can't take it more.' I said.

'It happens initially but letter on you will enjoy the same taste. Just go on.' Shyam laughed and said.

I closed my eyes and drunk one fourth of the bear glass. I felt that everything will come out. But I managed to control. Intoxication started in sometime and I felt like every nerves of my body going in relax mode.

'How are you feeling buddy?' Shyam said.

'I am feeling more better. I am enjoying.'

'Be steady. Always follow 3D rules while boozing. Dilution, Duration and Discussion' He said.

I smiled and my mind gave attention to third part more.

'You know, I still love her. Though I am trying to avoid her, but it's all because there is a single ray of hope left to get her.' I said.

'You will surely get her buddy if she will be in your destiny. Leave it on it.' Shyam said.

'Hey God! I can't show her, but I can assure You that nobody in this world can love her more than me.' I screamed.

Saurabh smiled and thought it as influence of liquor. But people who booze can very well understand that every word comes from deep corner of heart after intoxication.

'Sometimes I feel that she has something inside her heart for me but sometimes I doubt. Our great scientist must invent a machine to read the story going in a girl's heart.' I said.

Saurabh and Shyam smiled.

'It will be your job now. You are the sufferer, so you should take the responsibility to invent it.' Saurabh said.

I smiled. It was 10:05 pm. I felt my phone ringing. I took out the phone from my pocket. My phone's screen was showing 'Ritika...Calling'. I doubted my eyes and mind to be under the influence of liquor. I stressed my eyes and mind again but I could see the same name. I went out of the room in panic and received the call.

'Hello" I said.

'Hi Raghav, Ritika here. Where are you?'

[Statuary Warning: Drinking is Injurious to Health.]

, 'At my room.'

'I am in extreme need. Can you come to Charbagh railway station within half an hour? '

'Of course I will but what happened?'

'I will tell you when you will meet. Give me a call after reaching there.'

'Right.'

I felt coming in my own senses. I hugged Shyam and Saurabh.

'What happened?' Saurabh asked.

'Guys, I have received a call from Ritika. She wants me to meet at Charbagh. She didn't tell the reasons.'

'Ritika? At this time? I can't believe.' Shyam wondered.

'You can see the call details if you have doubt. I have to leave now.' I said.

I brushed my mouth to kill the smell of beer and took the auto for charbagh. I again received the call.

'Where are you?' She asked.

"I am in auto. It will take hardly 10 to 15 minutes to reach there.'

'Okay, I have parked my car near the stand. Come.'

'Yes, I am coming.'

I reached there and saw Ritika at the driving seat and her mother was lying on the back seats.

'Raghav, she fell, down while walking with me suddenly. We have to rush to the hospital. Just hold my mother so that she does not fall from the seats.'

I held her mother and she started the car.

'I placed her inside with the help of my servant. Actually his wife has gone at her in-laws home. Papa went to Delhi yesterday for official works. I did not want my servant to be with me at this time. So I…' She said.

'No issue.' I said.

We reached to the hospital and attendants took her to the emergency. Ritika briefed the doctor about her. Her B.P. was too low. They gave her medicines and an injection and started glucose. Around 12:15 am she felt normal. We were sitting beside her.

'Mumma how are you feeling now?' She asked.

'Comfortable. You had your dinner?' Her mother asked.

'Yes I had.'

'Who is he?' She asked in a uncomfortable way.

'He is Raghav from my class. Nobody was thereto accompany me so I called him.'

'Where are you from?' her mother asked to me.

'From Azamgarh aunty.' I said.

'Where do you live in Lucknow?'

'Near our university.' I said.

'You had your dinner?'

'Yes aunty I had.'

I felt her mother of being so caring nature. But who cares for food when you are with a girl to whom you love more than your life. I did not feel appetite even after boozing.

'Do you want to have tea?' Ritika asked.

'Yes but where we will get at this time.'

''There is a canteen which remains open 24 hrs. Mumma we are going to have tea. Let's go.'

We went to the canteen and sat beside each other.

'How is your fiance?' I asked.

'Don't discuss about him. I don't want to spoil my mood.'

'So you don't want to share with me.'

'It's not like that but here I don't want to discuss.'

'It's okay. No issue.'

Though it's so difficult to ask a girl to whom you love about a boy to whom she loves but I wanted to know about their relationship and my chance to make another entry in her life. I felt happy knowing her reaction for his fiancé.

'You play well' she said.

'It's my passion.' I said.

'That's great. I love to play basketball. I got many trophies during my schooling.'

'Wow. Beautiful. You have good height.'

'What did you had in your dinner?'

'Actually, I could not have because we were preparing when I received your call.'

'Oh , I am so sorry. I am having biscuits and some snacks in my bag. Let me bring.'

She tried to leave the seat but I held her arms and said;

'Ritika please sit. I don't have appetite.'

I felt of a liquid flowing through every nerve of my body and intoxication the whole system. Her face expression changed.

She sat on the chair looking on the floor. We kept silent for some movement. Her eyes met with me but neither she nor me could tell anything.

Canteen boy asked us to take tea from counter.

'Your eyes look reddish. Are you feeling sleepy?' She asked.

'I don't feel so. I am okay.' I said.

'Everything is fine at your home?'

'Yes normal.'

'You looks so serious. Are you not comfortable?' She asked.

'No it's not like that. I am tired little bit.' I said.

'I can understand.'

We had tea, we went to her mother. We could hardly sleep. I made myself comfortable on a vacant bed near her. Doctor told us to take her home in the morning. Though I wanted to go her home but I pretended to know her reaction.

'You drop me at Charbagh then I will go by auto.'

'No, I will drop you near IT crossing. It will take hardly 15 minutes.'

But she did not tell to take me at her home. She dropped me.

'See you Raghav. Thanks a lot.'

'See you bye. Bye Auntie.'

She left. I walked to my room.

'Welcome our hero. What happened yesterday. We were trying your number but it was out of reach' Shyam asked.

I told them the whole story.

'If she does not want to keep relationship with you then why she called you for help?' Shyam again asked.

'The same question is running in my mind. God knows only. And you know how did she behaved with me after my proposal and today she was asking that why I was so serious with her. Girls are too difficult to understand.' I said.

'Girls are so clever man. You will learn slowly. They want everything from us. Though they have the same feeling but they never tell so that they can claim in future that you went behind not she.' Shyam said.

'You are so experienced man.' I said.

'They look very innocent but they have very intelligent mind. That's why intelligence agencies are preferring to recruit women employees.' Shyam said.

I laughed and Shyam again reacted,

'Don't laugh buddy. It's true. A gents officer needs hours to take out something from a culprit while a lady officer needs a minute.'

We all laughed and went to have tea.

ONE MONTH LATER

15th October this year 2015, 11:00 pm.

It was a day before of her birthday. I was in dilemma that weather I should wish her or not. Wishing her was a big issue because it would finish my current attitude with her and I will be again biased to have relationship with her.

I tried to control myself but I could not. I typed a message;

'Wish you a very happy birthday. May God give you lot of joy and happiness. Enjoy the day.'

I sent it and got a delivery report. I waited for her reply but I didn't get. I managed to sleep and woke up by 07:15 am. My eyes straight went on my cell. It was flashing a message.

'It's so nice of you Raghav. I am feeling happy that you remember it. I will not come to faculty today due to bad health of my mother. We will have treat on some other day.'

'It's okay. Take care of your mother and have a nice day.' I replied.

I went to the faculty and attended the class. I was much excited to know her reaction on my birthday on 20th October. On 19th Saurabh asked;

'So tomorrow again you want to celebrate your fake birthday?'

'Of course buddy. I enjoy in doing something different.' I said.

'So you will celebrate it with our Bhabhi Ji?' Shyam asked.

'No, I will not go to faculty. We will have party at evening.' I smiled and said.

'Oh, It's heartening. You should also invite her for party.'

'Who cares if she is not interested.' I pretended.

I was eagerly waiting my watch to show 1200 am. I was expecting a message from her but I was in doubt because of her mother's illness. My screen flashed with a message at 11:58 pm by my watch.

'Happy birthday bro.' from Chintamani.

I said him thanks. At 12:10 by my watch I again received a message. It was from Ritika.

'Many happy returns of the day Raghav. Can you give me some of your precious time tomorrow?'

'Thanks. Of course I can but what for? and where?' I replied.

'I want to meet you at CCD in Ganj at 04:00 pm.'

'Okay. You will not come for class today?'

'No. See you there. Bye.'

'Bye'

I woke up by 06:45 am. I felt very happy and was excited to meet her. I did not go to faculty. I was much curious. I dressed up well and went little early to become familiar of that place. I went inside the Café and read the menu. I called Ritika and told her that I had reached. She told me that it will take 10 minutes more to reach her. We sat facing each other.

'Happy birthday.' She said.

'Thank you' I replied.

'What would you like to have?' She asked.

'As you like. Nothing special.'

She ordered coffee and snacs.

'Today I am giving you treat but your will be due. Don't forget.' She said.

'It's okay. How is your mother now?' I asked.

'Not so good but better.'

'Did you tell your father about that day?'

'It's of no use. He will not do anything. I know him.'

'That is pathetic.'

'He came with Shruti on night before my birthday. I felt upset, so did not celebrate.'

'Your mother did not see her.'

'No, I can see from my room's window. My mother's room is inside.'

'Oh God! Which type of peoples you send to this world sometimes.'

'Anyway leave it. I am spoiling your mood. It's your birthday. You should be happy.'

Meanwhile, I collected the coffee and snacks from the counter. It was my first coffee with her and at CCD. I thought that if some where question will be asked that with whom you had you first coffee at CCD, then I will proudly say her name. I did not like its taste. I thought that these peoples should go and learn from my mother to prepare it.

She opened her purse and take out a gift.

'It's my gift on your birthday. Please do not let others to open it.' She said.

'Something secret?' I asked.

'Not only secret but top secret.' she said.

I could not understand what happened to her but she started looking at me. I diverted my eyes from her. A drops of water came out of her eyes.

'What happened?' I asked.

'Nothing'

'Then why are you too low?'

'I am feeling relaxed and happy. I want to leave now. My mother is lonely at home.' She said.

'Yes you should.'

She went and I took auto to reach to my room. I was much excited to open the gift. I locked the room then opened it. There were three items. A birthday greeting card, a fast track watch with long dial and an envelope with an A-4 size paper, written.

"Hey my sweet heart,

It's too difficult to hide the facts for me now. I want you to hear my true inner vice today. I truly, heartly, honestly and badly love you. I want you to lock inside my heart so that no one can snatch you from me.

I don't know the reasons but I feel my life is incomplete without you. From very first day, when I saw your innocent face, I felt something different. I always feel happy and secure with you.

When you proposed me, I could not sleep for many nights. My heart didn't take even a single second to decide that I should tell you, 'I do more than you.' But I tried to follow my mind.

You know the condition of my family. I did not want to take any decision in haste which would ruin our life like my parents.

I wanted more time to judge you but I thought you will not be able to give me. Keeping stone my heart, I told you everything on that day.

But today I want to tell you that I am your Ritika. I was waiting for your birthday to come. I thought it as a best day to tell you the truth."

An enzyme of internal happiness ran throughout my body. My feets wanted to leave the earth. I started dancing inside the room, though I had never done. I kissed that letter, card and watch many times.

I went to Shyam and told him the whole story. He lifted me in the air and left. They both came to my room and saw the gift. Though it was my fake birthday but it had become most valuable day of my life.

I called the Ritika in the evening. She picked up the phone. We were silent for some movement.

'Hello...oooo' She said.

'Yes' I said.

We again went in silent for some movement.

'Say something.' She said.

'You cheated me.'

'Why?'

'You should have told me the facts and if at all you had problem, you could have discussed me.'

'I am so sorry. But I took decision keeping in mind for our better future.'

'It's so simple for you to say sorry but you can't understand how much I paid for this. You can't imagine, how could I survived after your rejection. Not even a single day was passed without remembering you.'

'Really? But you looked normal always.'

'That is the problem, nobody understand the internal wounds. You would have seen if I had external. You girls leave the boys straight way.'

'Oh, you are so experienced. With how many girls you had relationship in the past?'

'Not with a single one.'

'So from where you got these experiences?'

'I live in a society. I have too many friends.'

'It's too painful to know that your friends always got bullshit from girls.'

'I don't know. You have given me a lot of pain. You have to pay for it first.'

'Oh how much rupees you want tell. I am having a big heart. Ask freely.'

I laughed silently and said.

'I am not kidding. I am serious. I want a date with you.'

'Oh really so now I am also serious. So date with me is '16th October 15 with Ritika Rai'

I kept silent. She felt that I am angry. She told then;

'I am sorry, seriously. Tell me, where do you want to go with me.'

'At place where you and me will be only.'

'Hey do you want to kill me at that place? Anyway coming Saturday. Are u free?'

'Always for you.'

'That's so sweet of you. We will have dinner at Dhaba on Lucknow Sultanpur highway.'

'You have had food there?'

'Yes but once. I was going to Sultanpur by bus with my maternal uncle. It was too tasty.'

'Okay, I am surprised to know that a daughter of an IRS officer would like to have dinner at Dhaba.'

'C' 'mon don't make a joke. These little happiness's make our life enjoyable.'

'That's why I love you. You are so simple.'

'Okay bye now, I have to do lot of jobs.'

'Bye. Take care.'

On coming Saturday, She came to pick me with her car by 05:15 pm. It was little bit cold outside.

'Where are we going?' I asked.

'We don't have any destination. We will keep on going.' she said.

"Wow you are following the song 'Musafir hoon mai yaron na ghar hai na thikana, bus yuhin chalte jana."

'That is beautiful song. I love it.'

'You are looking so pretty.'

'Seriously?'

'I don't joke every time like you.'

'Thank you from core of my heart.'

"Do you use beauty products to look better?"

'Sometimes, but I love perfumes and sprays.'

'That I know from very first day, you sat just in front me.'

'That's nice and what more you know about me?'

'Your neck is so beautiful.'

She smiled.

'I am feeling scared now going with you lonely. You are not as innocent as you look.'

'I don't know.'

She turned the car for highway. I badly wanted to take a tea. She stopped the car on a tea shop. Though it was a small shop but outside environment was too beautiful. There were lots of plants and flowers outside. We sat on the hard bed. A cold breeze was moving. We ordered the tea.

'Yes Miss Ritika, what would you like to pay today for pains you gave me?' I asked.

'I think Rupees 1000 will be more than sufficient for you.'

Though I wanted to ask her seriously but I pretended to be in kidding mood. Sometimes we ask something in kidding mood to know the reaction from apposite, so that if you get negative response, then also things will not be as much serious as asking it seriously. But if a person apposite to you also give a kidding answer then your plan fails.

'And how these thousand rupees will take away my pain?'

'Just go and watch movies. Eat the food you want and roam here and there.'

'I hardly get happiness and enjoy in these things.'

'Oh then you should go in the company of our's spiritual Baba to get internal happiness. You can reach to them also in Rs 1000'

'Anyway give me Rs 1000 first.'

'Very clever. First you plan and workout where to go, pay from your pocket, give me the bills, then I will pay to you.'

I touched her ears and twisted.

'Will you give me or not?'

'Not so easily'

I twisted more. She reacted.

'Please leave, I will...Surely I will.'

Then I released. Her face expression changed. It became serious. I felt something different after touching her ears. We kept silent for next five minutes. We finished our tea in between and left the shop.

It was dark outside. Ritika switched on the headlights. After moving 500 meters she took the car aside and stopped.

'What happened?' I asked.

'Raghav what do you want me to pay?'

'C'mon , 'I was just kidding.' I said.

'No, I know you were not kidding.'

'Believe me. I wanted to know your reaction.'

'No tell me seriously.'

'Then just come and sit near me for some movement.'

We both went on the rear seat. We sat close to each other. I kept my hands over her and made a grip. She also helped in it. Our faces turned to each other automatically. After that I could not remember where I am. I lost my mind, my sense and my body inside her. I closed my eyes and placed over her. I touched my forehead with her. I place my nose over her. Then I kept my lips over her and kept away. She resisted. She placed her hands on my neck and her lips over mine and started eating it in such a way that she has got her favorite dish.

We kept on doing but her phone started ringing. It was her mother's call.

'Hello mumma'

'Where are you beta.'

'Mumma, There is a long traffic jam at Charbagh. I will reach soon as soon it clears.'

'Okay. Drive slow. I am okay.'

'Ok, See you.'

We came to front seats and she said to me;

'Raghav we have to expedite now. There is a Dhaba just one kilometer from here.'

'Yes off course.'

We kept silent till reaching the Dhaba. We ordered Dal, Roti and Sabji.

Then I said, 'You paid today'

'You look innocent but you are too much clever from inside, I came to know today.' She said.

'So you mean to say innocent people don't have heart and mind.'

'Exactly, they should not have.'

'Very funny. When you are going to meet me next.'

'Enjoy today. Don't think for tomorrow.'

Meanwhile waiter brought the diner. We sat cross legged on hard bed and had the tasty food. As she was in hurry I asked her to drop me at Charbagh only. I took auto and came to my room.

I received a call at same night from her at 10:30 pm.

'Yes Mr Raghav, how are you?' She asked.

'Fine Mrs Raghav, you should stop calling me by name?' I replied.

'OMG, you are going beyond permissible speed. Slow down otherwise you will have accident and why I should stop calling your name?'

'You don't know, In our culture wives do not pronounce their husband's name.'

'Stop all this non-sense.'

'I will continue.'

'Meet me then I will see how do you do this.'

'What will you do?'

'I will bring a tape with hard fixing gum and will put it on your lips so that you will not be able to speak.'

'So you want to eat the tapes instead of my lips. I was not knowing that you like the taste of gum and tapes.'

'Don't go so deep Mr It's too early.'

'Hey, I forgot to ask you that you were in relationship? What happened?'

'It was all non-sense which I did with you like you are doing with me. I thought that If I will simply refuse you then you may try to reach me again.'

'Very nice. God should do brain drain from girls to boys.'

'God will never do. He knows that boys will misuse it always.'

'Leave. How did you feel today?'

'I liked cold breeze at the tea shop and having tea there. I loved driving on highway. It's my passion.'

'I was with you, It didn't meant for you. You could have enjoyed lonely with cold breeze and driving.'

'That I don't want to discuss.'

'That is the basic problem with girls. They never clarify the things and whenever they become unable to reply they don't want to discuss.

'It's not the thing to discuss. It can be felt only. Feelings once discussed will be lost from your heart.'

'God knows. I can't understand this weird thought. Tell me what is your perception about love.'

'It's a type of feeling for a person, place or thing to which you don't want to leave at any cost.'

'But what about physical relations involved in it.'

'It's all disgusting.'

'So why you involved in it?'

'That I don't want to discuss.'

I smiled and told,

'But I want to discuss. It's not fair that the things which you like will be discussed always.'

'Shut up. Tell me you perception now.'

'For me it's a condition in which you loose your mind, you starts following your heart and you become the foolish one.'

'Very nice but from where you got these experiences?'

'From a girl who is talking with me right now and she will be very happy after knowing this.'

'Oh you read my mind.' She smiled and told.

'You girls never ever think of condition of boys after your rejection. You should have sympathy at least.'

'If I would have shown sympathy to you then you would have tried to reach me again.'

'Very funny. Means you should leave them straightway.'

'See you people don't have control on your emotions but girls know very well to control it and they take decisions after balancing their heart and mind.'

'So you should teach boys to keep control as a part your sympathy after rejection.'

'Okay it will be monitored next time.'

'Next time? You will do again like that.'

'No, I am just kidding.'

'I will shoot you if you will do it again.'

'It's 11:10 pm by my watch. You don't want to sleep?'

'Who want to sleep while talking with a girl for whom he never slept for many nights?'

'That's so sweet of you. But I want to sleep now.'

'Very clever! You want to sleep but you are asking me to sleep.'

'I am feeling sleepy now. Bye Gdnt.'

'Bye.'

I received a call from her at 0700 pm next Saturday.

'Hello, Where are you?' She asked.

'At my room. Tell'

'Actually mumma's B.P. is too low again. I have given him the medicine. Though it is recovering but I may require to take her to hospital. Can you come?'

'Off course, I will reach within 45 minutes'.

'Don't come in hurry. Do you know the location of my home?'

'Yes I visited Chintamani's home once. Then he showed me your home.'

'Very good. You are more forward than expected.'

'Okay see you soon.' I smiled and told.

I dressed up well, reached to her home and knocked the bell. She came and took me to show her home first.

'Where is mumma?' I asked?

'She is sleeping in her room' She said.

It was four room well-furnished home with modular kitchen and balcony. Different rooms were painted in different colors and styles. Whole floor was made of white marble. There were six window Ac's installed at different locations.

She took me to drawing room and asked me to sit. Lady servant brought the water and asked for tea or coffee? Ritika told her that she herself will prepare. Two pots with money plants were kept near sofa. Lights were looking like of modern showrooms. Trophies were kept in upper rack of cupboard.

'It's a beautiful house. Whose trophies are these?'

'Except two all are mine. I got these for winning basketball matches, debates and for 1st positions during my schooling. I will show you my album but first let me prepare a coffee for you.'

'That's great. Can I see you while preparing coffee for you?'

'No not at all, men's are not allowed inside the kitchen.'

'Oh, its ok then , I will sit here only.'

'No..No, come, I was kidding.'

I loved watching her while preparing coffee for me standing on the doors of her kitchen. She prepared and we went inside her mamma's room. She introduced me and gave her a cup of coffee. We had the coffee and after that she measured her B.P.

It was better than previous. We again came back to drawing room.

'So how is your life going on?'

'You are in my life, I can't expect more from it.'

'That's so sweet of you.'

·'I want to hug you'

She was in such a nice and sweet mood that she straightway stood up, closed the doors, opened her arms and said,

'C'mon my innocent baby, I too want to hug you tightly.'

I loved her way of calling me. I can't forget that movement. We hugged each other. Our souls met with each other's. I felt drops of water on my neck.

'Hey what happened?' I asked.

'Nothing. I am relaxed. Just hold me tightly. Don't leave me. I never got such support. It's a great feeling.'

My lips touched her neck. I kissed. Then we sat on sofa.

'I feel so lonely. You know the story of my family. I am worried for mumma's health and our life ahead.'

'Do you have faith on me?'

'Off course I have but you are also depended on your family.'

'I will stand by you everywhere that much I know.'

'It's so sweet of you.'

'I thought that you are strong from inside.'

'Yes I try to look so to face the society and peoples.'

'Which type of heart your father has, I am not able to understand. You are the only daughter of him and how can he behave like this with you?'

'I don't know. I believe in Karma Philosophy. Do you know?'

'No, I don't know.'

'Good deeds pay you and you pay for your bad deeds. He will pay for her bad deeds one day.'

'That's great.'

'It's 8.00 pm by my watch I am going to prepare dinner. You sit and watch the T.V.'

'First go and measure the B.P. again.'

She went and checked her mother's B.P. It was close to normal. She went towards her lady servant's room for dinner arrangements. Meanwhile my phone started ringing. It was call from Saurabh.

'Hello Raghav where are you?'

'At Charbagh, tell.'

'Actually Shyam had a accident by his bike near I.T. There is a fracture in his left arm. I am at Vivekananda Polyclinic in NishatGanj.'

'Oh Shit , You be there, I am coming.'

Life gives you some type of situation in which your mind goes in dilemma. My one corner of heart was not allowing me to leave her and another wanted to be with my friend who was in need. I told whole story to Ritika. She herself advised me to go. We hugged each other once again and I left her home in hurry.

I reached at the hospital. We and Saurabh met with doctor again. He told us that he will apply POP on Shyam's left hand. We asked the doctor for pain killer as he was looking restless. He told us that he has already given.

'Should we inform his family?' Saurabh asked.

'No it's not required. We are here to take care of him. Let him be normal first.'

'Okay'

It was 10:30 p.m. when he interacted with us in normal voice.

'I am sure, a beautiful girl would be going on the road and you would have lost your concentration.' I said.

'No man. She was an old lady who was trying to overtake city bus.' Shyam said.

I smiled.

'Bad luck man. Accident do not matter but there must be a beautiful girl colliding with your vehicle. Then it will be memorable one.' I said.

'I don't have so good luck as you.'

'So, is she stopped after this?'

'Yes, she took me to the hospital also. Then I told her to dial Saurabh's number.'

'That's nice.'

'She gave two thousands rupees also.'

'Oh, that's too nice. It means she was good by heart.'

'Yes. What did doctor told to you both?'

'He will apply POP on your hand.'

'It's too pathetic to be in the hospital.'

'I know but you don't have options. Need not to worry, we are here for your time pass.'

Doctor applied POP. We and Saurabh took care of Shyam's need. The old lady also came to see him next day. And more exciting thing was that Ritika also came to see Shyam. She interacted with them. After one week we took him to our room.

Shyam wanted to go home because she needed more care. I accompanied him by train to his home at Shahjahanpur. Her mother and sister were socked after watching him. I told them the whole story. Next day I came back to Lucknow.

TWO MONTHS LATER

Shyam recovered and came back to Lucknow. I remember the date, It was 12th January. Shyam suddenly came out of his room and said;

'Raghav, there is a function at Shyam's home. We have to go there.'

'Today?' I wondered and asked.

'Yes.' Saurabh said.

'Why did he not told us in advance?'

'Hey buddy, I am sorry but it was not confirmed. A family is coming to see my sister for marriage. We have to go.' Shyam came out of room and said.

'You are great. When will we leave?' I asked.

'As soon as possible.' Shyam said.

'You are unique piece in the world.' I said.

We all dressed up soon and left our room to reach Charbagh railway station. We boarded the train for Shahjahanpur. There was no network in my cell. I searched for it many times but still problem existed. I opened my cell and took out the sim to reset it but network could not be selected.

'Hey guys, I am not able to select network on my cell.' I said.

'Oh, there is a problem with network in BSNL. I was trying to call my maternal uncle but his number is also switched off. Wait, It will be rectified' Shyam said.

'But I want to make a call to inform Ritika that I am going with you guys.' I said.

'I have switched off my cell. I am fed up with a girl. As soon I will switch it on, her call will come. Kindly wait for an hour or till reaching to home, then you can talk. Her class will be over and after reaching at her home he will not call.' Shyam said.

'I don't have balance right now Raghav.' Saurabh said.

'You all are poor peoples.' I said.

Saurabh went and brought coffee from a station. We had it having normal conversation. But I was worrying thinking that she may try to call on my number.

We reached at Shyam's home by 03:30 pm. His sister opened the door. I could not feel that peoples are coming to see her because of her normal costumes. We had refreshment and Saurabh asked;

'Let's go to the first floor.'

We went inside a room at first floor. Saurabh locked the door from inside. They both looked very serious and sat on the bed. I asked;

'What happened?'

'Raghav, something wrong has happened but it's not an end of life. You have to face it.'

'What?'

'Ritika and her family is no more.' Shyam said.

My feets started trembling. I raised my voice and said;

'What? I will slap you if you will do such type joke with me.'

'It's true.' Saurabh said.

I snatched his collar and said;

'Don't do such type of joke with me, I will kill you here only.'

Shyam came between us and said;

'Raghav leave him. It's true. You have to accept it.'

I slapped him very strongly.

'You kill both of us but it's true.' Shyam said.

I lost my own senses. My mind went in its lowest point of depression.

'Who told you both these non-senses?' I asked.

'Raghav see it's today's newspaper' Saurabh said.

I snatched it from him and read;

'A revenue officer Shot down his wife, daughter and then himself.'

I saw Ritika's and her mother's blurred photo in inset. My mind, my heart, my soul was not accepting it.

'No it can't be true. No one can snatch my love from me. Hey god where are you? You can't do such a big sin with me.'

I hit my head on the wall to take out blood from it. They took me away from the wall. I pushed them away.

'You both are the biggest enemy. Don't come near me.'

I lost control from myself. I find myself helpless. My whole body was trembling. My heart beat was at its maximum level. I begged to them;

'You both have done the greatest sin of the world. Why did you take me here? Please help me. I am begging you for my love. I wanted to see her. Please take me there.'

'Raghav please try to understand. Nothing is there. Bodies will be in postmortem house.' Saurabh said.

'Then take me there only. I will touch the feet of officer's there to see her. Otherwise, I will kill myself.' I screamed.

'They will catch you and put you inside the cell. They are not a such good human being. They are corps. They will torcher you to take out something from you. We broke your Sim card and placed an expired sim there. Otherwise they would have track you by taking out the call details of her phone.' Shyam said.

'I can face anything but I can't live without her.'

'Please understand Raghav, they will not allow you to see her. Who are you for them moreover?' Saurabh said.

I went towards the door. I tapped strongly on the lock by my hand. Shyam caught me and held me strongly.

'Please control yourself otherwise you will lost your mind.' Shyam said.

'Shoot me, if you both want to do fever for me. What for I should be alive? I have lost everything.' I said.

'It's not an end of your life. With time, everything will be normal. Believe me. Try to keep patience.' Saurabh said.

'Hey God! You can't be so cruel with me. I don't want to live.'

'There are your parents, your sister, your younger brothers. All depends on you. Where will they go if you will kill yourself? Don't be selfish. You can't quit for your comfort.'

'I can't imagine my life without her. Nobody has right to kill my love. If I would have aware of it then I would have killed that devil earlier.' I screamed.

Saurabh sat with me and Shyam went to the ground floor locking the door from outside. He brought the water. He gave me to drink but I poured the whole on my head.

Shyam's family was aware of my case. At evening her sister came to me and said;

'Bhaiya, I am with you. Don't worry. Time is running. Thing will be normal slowly with time.'

Drops of water started coming out of my eyes. Her eyes were also wet. Her voice gave me a support. She sat with me for half an hour and left.

TWO WEEKS LATER

I could not sleep for an hour even. I was completely restless. Shyam gave me the sleeping pills but It did not work. My mind was going in more and more unstable condition day by day. Saurabh and Shyam decided to take me to my home. They accompanied me and we all three went to my home.

They told the whole story to my father. Drops of water started coming out of my mother's eyes. Day by day I started forgetting the things. I was not able to remember weather I took food or not weather I took bath or not. I could not remember the dates even.

My father took me to a hospital. I met with a physiatrist. He asked me the whole story. I was not able to speak. My father gave him the history of my illness. I got admitted and sister gave me an anti-psychotic injection.

I don't know due to its side effect or some other reasons, my restlessness increased. I was not able to sit on my bed. I wanted to roam every time. I felt more abnormal. After one hour of injection, I went in sound sleep. I could not remember what happened with me in next three days. My sister told me that I could woke up only for taking food and natural call. Doctor diagnosed me as a case of 'Major Depressive disorder'. After three days I felt comfortable than previous. Doctor started giving me anti-psychotic medicine. I was in acute ward. There were lots of severe patients too. A patient was talking laying on the bed without phone or any medium.

I asked 'To whom you are talking?'

'He replied 'Reply is coming from there and I am talking with her. You should not listen my talk. Go, it's a something private.'

I felt scared and thought of getting well soon. Due to medicines I always felt sleepy. My family did not take proper food due to my condition. I recovered slowly and got discharge after a month. I came to home. My father told me that Shyam and Saurabh called him daily to know my condition. They came to meet me. Shyam's sister talked me·to on phone and consoled me. My mother kept on giving me medicine on time.

My memory recovered by the medicine. Not even a single day was passed without remembering her. My mother used to tell me daily something good about my life. I went to the market, there I saw 'Ritika Coffee Bar'. I had seen this shop many times before also but this time it made more impact on my mind. I had a coffee there and asked the man on the counter.

'Who is Ritika?'

'She is my daughter studying in fourth standard.'

'That's so sweet.' I said.

I purchased a packet of chocolate from same shop and asked her father to give her from my side. Though, she is not with me today but I celebrate her birthday and my fake birthday every year.

———— x x x x x ————